How to Deal with
FRiENDS

Words by Richard Powell
Pictures by Alan Snow

MALLARD
PRESS

When I was little, my mom took me to meet some children who played together. "Here are some friends for you to play with," she said. She didn't tell me that sometimes . . .

they were rough . . .

I would have to share . . .

they got mad . . .

they wouldn't play at all.

But now we're bigger, and we've all learned
to be friends — most of the time. We play amazing
games together. Here are some things that happened
to me when I was making friends . . .

"Get off my foot!"

These are my friends. George, John, Pat, Tom, and Barker.
George is the largest.
John is the youngest.
Pat is the oldest.

"Woof!"

Tom is the naughtiest.
Barker is a dog.
He is my best friend.

"Mom, when are they going?"

When I first met George, I was shy. Mom said
to go outside and play. I didn't want to. She said:
"Show George your new bike."
So I did.

"It's a brand-new red bike, you know."

It's a great bike.
George thought so, too.
I let George ride it.
We soon became friends.

"It's *my* bike."

Sometimes I don't like people riding my bike.
I pushed Pat off it once and made her cry.
I was sorry I did that.
I bandaged her knee with some toilet paper.

"I want to play with Teddy."

Pat played with Teddy. I wanted to play with Teddy. I pulled on Teddy's leg so hard it came off. Mom said we should take turns with Teddy. We think she's right. So does Teddy.

"Do you have any more red?"

John came to play the other day.
I let him share my paints.
He gave me some of his chocolate.
We painted a pretty picture together.

"Give me that car!"

George and John came to play with me.
George is big. John is small.
George kept pushing John over and making him cry.
I don't think that was very nice.

"Cheat!"

"Let's play hide-and-seek," I said one day to Tom and John, who had come to play. Tom and I went to hide, but John cheated. He kept looking through his fingers and finding us right away.

"Try cheating *now*!"

"I've got x-ray eyes," he said. Tom and I got mad. Tom got a bucket and put it over John's head. We got into trouble. The bucket had water in it. We should have talked it over.

"We are pirates. Hooray!"

My mom says you shouldn't do things to others that you wouldn't like done to yourself.

"I don't like playing pirates."

I think she's right.

On my birthday I invited my friends to a party.

We played all kinds of games.

We ate lots of food.

It was a great party.

"Zoom!"

But sometimes I like to play on my own . . .

"Heel, Barker, heel!"

or with my dog, Barker. He has to do what he's told.

But playing with all my friends is a lot of fun, too!